T0197001

A Living Sacrifice

TrUe ReAl

A LIVING SACRIFICE

iUniverse books may be ordered through booksellers or by contacting:

iUniverse
1663 Liberty Drive
Bloomington, IN 47403
www.iuniverse.com
1-800-Authors (1-800-288-4677)

Because of the dynamic nature of the Internet, any web addresses or links contained in this book may have changed since publication and may no longer be valid. The views expressed in this work are solely those of the author and do not necessarily reflect the views of the publisher, and the publisher hereby disclaims any responsibility for them.

This is a work of fiction. All of the characters, names, incidents, organizations, and dialogue in this novel are either the products of the author's imagination or are used fictitiously.

Any people depicted in stock imagery provided by Getty Images are models, and such images are being used for illustrative purposes only. Certain stock imagery © Getty Images.

ISBN: 978-1-5320-4727-5 (sc)
ISBN: 978-1-5320-4728-2 (e)

Library of Congress Control Number: 2018905135

Print information available on the last page.

iUniverse rev. date: 05/03/2018

Contents

Plot Line: (A Living Sacrifice)

The story begins in beautiful Key West, Florida where the money rolls and champagne flows freely. Casper is a well-established business man by day. Jennifer is an up and coming lawyer in the firm who has everything but a one true love. Maurice is Casper's twin brother who's a well-established business lawyer but thrives on the darker side of the law. Taco & Tara are brother and sister who has built their career around decent in getting the job done at any cost. Candi was once a stripper, build her empire by becoming a high-class Madam who loves to feed the delight of any sexual desires but at a high cost.

So, sit back and watch the highly sexual intensity, mind blowing, erotic life of "A Living Sacrifice"

The meeting

Casper meets with Taco and Maurice; the shipment is late and they do not need any further problems. "Do not worry brother, I will handle it" Maurice says as he leaves the room, leaving Casper and Taco to discuss the issues at hand. Casper tells Taco to handle this himself because Maurice is soft and to keep a close eye on him YES sir.

"Good afternoon baby" Casper says to Jennifer. "I thought you had forgotten about me" she says. "No Jennifer, you have been on my mind all day long. Why don't we go outside and have lunch, how about a picnic"? "Yes, baby, that sounds great". Casper takes Jennifer to a private spot on his estate and as they talk he asks Jennifer to do something for him, she says "anything Casper" as she holds him wanting him to kiss her deeply, badly. He pins her down slightly, sliding her strapped clothing to the side, eventually ripping them off her body, forcing him to go hard into her flesh. As he holds back from releasing what she wants inside her, he kisses and bites her upper lip telling her "you're mine" as he releases his soldiers into her naked body like an army gone wild.

Casper gets up, his phone ringing, and after this short conversation tells her that he needs to leave town. "I will call you soon baby", she turns over violated and loving every minute of it she falls asleep with tears in her eyes.

{Scene opens with Casper sitting on his plush black leather sofa looking visibly angry while talking on his cellphone yelling.}

Casper screams into the phone "I'M GOING TO KILL MAURICE". An older male voice on the other end says "You don't mean that". Casper, still yelling, "I MEAN IT, THIS TIME HE'S GONE TOO FAR". Male voice chuckles, "Calm down and tell me what's wrong". Casper explains "I'm supposed to be in charge of this operation, right"? Male voice, "Son, you boys promised me before I left that you could handle the business". Casper tries to argue "but Dad...." Dad raises his voice "Look damn it, there's too much at stake here for you and Maurice to fuck up now. Did you ship the package as ordered"? Casper, realizing Dad means business replies "yes, Sir". Dad, satisfied with Casper's answer, replies "good! Now I need. . . ." Casper suddenly interrupts his dad once he sees Traci entering the room. "I'll call you back". Casper hangs up and remaining calm asks Traci "What are you doing here"? Traci smiles as she plops down on the couch next to Casper. "Did you forget baby"? Casper yells "Forget what"? Traci slides to her knees and begins to unzip Casper's pants. "It's our anniversary baby, today's our anniversary". Casper, not in the mood for Traci's antics today, yells "Stop It! Look Traci we need to talk". Traci jumps up yelling

"WHAT CASPER?? IS IT BECAUSE OF THAT BITCH ASS JENNIFER SHIT AGAIN"? Casper rolls his eyes, "No, and please stop with the name calling, she's not a bitch". Traci places her well-manicured hand on her hip. "WHO IN THE FUCK GAVE YOU THE RIGHT TO TELL ME WHAT TO SAY OR NOT TO SAY"? Casper pulls Traci by the arm onto the couch and sighs, "Look baby, I'm sorry okay, it has nothing to do with Jennifer; it's my asshole of a brother, Maurice, who has me so upset". Traci, with a look of sadness, "Oh baby, I'm sorry, I just wish you would get out of the business. I have enough money to take care of the both of us". Casper slowly stands up tucking his shirt into his pants and zips up his pants. "It's not that simple. I got to go". Traci, visibly upset demands to know where he is going? Casper walks towards the door, "I need to clear my head".

Meanwhile Jennifer's in bed with a dazed look on her face when her cellphone rings.

Jennifer answers, "Hello"! It is Tyra, the accountant "Is everything ok"? Jennifer, still dazed replies "Yes, why"? Tara says "we were supposed to meet today. Where are you"?

Jennifer gasps. "Oh God, I completely forgot. Give me thirty minutes". Tyra receives an incoming call and hits the answer button on her phone. "Hello".

Taco informs Tyra the hit man made his flight and is scheduled to arrive at 9:30PM. "Do you have everything in place"? Tyra says "yes Sir". Ok I will call you after we leave the airport. Tyra reminds Taco, "Make sure he tells you everything". Taco laughs, "Don't worry he will. I know my uncle, he likes to brag".

Several hours later Casper returns to his penthouse; once inside he notices rose petals leading to his bedroom. He follows the trail and spots Traci in bed on her stomach wearing a black sheer teddy. Casper unzips his pants and removes his blue silk boxer shorts. He slowly crawls into bed while licking between Traci's muscular Ivory thighs until he reaches the crack of Traci's ass. Traci is awakened by the pleasure of Casper's long wet tongue wiggling into his tunnel. Casper whispers, "Get on your knees". Traci willingly follows his command as she arches her back and places her head on the fluffy down filled pillow.

Preaching the gospel Pastor Dew Right Cum for Me.

Scene opens with Candi, Key West's high class Madam, and Casper, well established business man standing in her high class erotic office. Candi informs him, "The deal will be sealed tonight". Casper walks towards the door to exit her office, "I'm on my way to France to see my friend and have some fun". Candi curiously asks, "Who Traci? You so nasty"! Casper flashes a quick smile as he slowly closes the door. Candi's assistant comes in shortly after he leaves, "Boss we are doing well tonight". Candi smiles, "let me know when my man gets here". Her assistant replies, "yes ma'am". Candi tells her to send him directly to her room. Minutes later, Pastor Dew Right enters. Candi's assistant with a smirk on her face asks him, "Hey Pastor how's it going"? Pastor Dew Right replies, "Fine, is Candi around"? She assures him that she is, "Yes sir"! Pastor Dew Right gives a quick wave as he walks in a fast pace to Candi's office. He opens the door as though he was swatting a huge fly, then slams the door, causing the pictures on the wall to shake, all while blurting out as though he was ending his Sunday sermon, "I NEED YOU BABY!!" Candi softly replies, with a smile in her voice, "Business before pleasure Pastor"! He replies sarcastically, "Oh I'm going to give you some business". Candi laughs out while unbuckling his chrome belt and unzipping his black creased pants as she raises her voice in excitement "DAMN PREACH THAT SHIT"! As she places her moist, juicy, ruby red lips onto his full Caramel right walnut while gently gliding her wet tongue against his extended rod and begins to pleasure him as though she was sucking on a ripe Georgia Peach, causing Pastor Dew Right to yell "YES LAWD, THIS SHIT FEELS GOOD"! He then places his strong manicured hand on the top of her head while slightly guiding her to his big long veiny rod as he yells out again, "DAMN BABY, NOTIFY THE CONGREGATION THAT I WANT TO BAPTIZE YOUR THROAT WITH MY MILK AND HONEY, PLEASE!!" Candi then grabs his firm thighs and motions him down to the floor and lays the Pastor on the floor in front of the fireplace and releases his manhood for a brief moment and licks her full smeared lips and whispers, "It's OK baby, Mama needs to feed you your formula". Pastor Dew Right slowly opens his mouth and whispers, "Candi baby, let me suck on your inner core". Candi slowly opens her legs as she bends towards his strong muscular face to straddle him as Pastor Dew Right begins to eat her. Candi embraces his tongue-lashing sermon, as she feels the word being spoken to her soul, she begins to tense up with natures flowing juices glistening down her thighs all while holding his face she says, "right their baby, that's the spot, lick the core out" she passionately blurts out "DAMN"! Pastor Dew Right begins to feel her soul as he forcefully slurp all around her glory. Suddenly he flips her over to her knees pulling her tightly and ridiculously while raising his dick as if a thunderstorm was Cumming. Candi arches her back as he guides his dick and begins to deliver his message into her and to speak life into her soul. Candi becomes so overwhelmed with the Pastor's message, she begins to shake and tremor, becoming overtaken by the spirit, causing her to speak in tongues. Pastor abruptly pushes her away and jumps to his feet while backing away with the look of horror and yells to the top of his lungs like a roaring lion; "LAWD WHAT HAVE I DONE"? Candi slowly rises while bellowing out a forced giggle and calmly says "great things baby, I'll meet you out back. Oh, but please, take this as my offering to you", as she softly kisses his chest before walking away.

What has transpired, and what is Casper up to, and who is his friend?

{Scene opens with Casper standing in Candi's office}

Casper is looking directly at Candi with great intensity in his eyes, "Well, how did the meeting go with the good Pastor"? Candi glances towards the fireplace with a smirk; replaying the tongue-lashing sermon from Pastor Dew Right, feeling a slight quiver inside her core from the memory of his mighty sword. She lets out a deep sigh. "Well boss, he touched my soul. He really gave me a soul-searching sermon". Casper nods his head with a look of relief". "Great! Well, I'll see you in a week". Walking towards the door he turns and smiles "do what you do baby."

Scene opens with Casper back at his high-rise penthouse that overlooks the city. He plops down onto his French leather, plush, black couch with his cellphone placed to his ear. Jennifer, the new up and coming lawyer, stands at her desk in a panic, gathering files for her first high profile case. She reaches for her phone with disgust in her voice, "HELLO". Casper, speaking softly and deeply, "Hey Baby". Jennifer gushes, "Oh Casper, baby

I missed you". Casper replies, "I've missed you too baby". Jennifer replies, "Baby, I'm sorry but I can't talk right now. I'm working on a big case". As Jennifer's office door opens, a male voice speaking loudly calls out, "we got to go or we're going to be late." Jennifer raises her well-manicured finger and whispers, "OK I'm coming", while speaking into the phone, "Casper, Baby, I got to go". Casper pleads, "Jennifer wait"! Jennifer, "Casper Please"! Casper, "Jennifer I Need You". Jennifer, looking with a great fear and shock in her eyes, while staring into the eyes of her angry assistant, bellows out "I'm sorry, tell my secretary I'm not to be disturbed". The assistant throws his hands up in disgust and slams the door. Jennifer "Casper, baby what's wrong"? Casper, "Sit down and open your legs". Jennifer yells, "WHAT"? Casper leans forward into the phone, raising his voice, while speaking slowly, "Open your legs and touch my peach firmly in your hand, and play with the outer side of your grace". Jennifer, while slowly raising her right leg onto her marble desk whispers as she falls to his commands, "Baby, no". Casper whispers, "Close your eyes and softly flicker your finger across your cherry", Jennifer complies, as she feels the moisture glide onto her finger as she becomes aroused from the hardening of her cherry. She begins to moan in her delight. Casper becomes increasingly aroused from her sweet moans, causing his manhood to rise to the occasion. He requests her to go deeper. Jennifer raises her pelvis, motioning herself back and forth feeling the tightness pressing on her finger. Casper, "faster baby, faster". Jennifer reaches for her once treasured gavel that sits on her desk and begins to insert the thick wood into her extremely wet throbbing garden; gliding it in and out becoming more aroused by the sound of the gushing of her juices. Casper, gripping his hardening rod, becomes distracted by the sound of a door closing and footsteps coming closer. He begins to motion his finger towards his needs. Feeling a wet tongue and firm lips begin to engulf a rhythm to his throbbing. Casper, "Oh Yes". Jennifer responds to his pleasure by delighting herself, causing her to increase the pain of her stroke by going faster and harder pushing her pelvis to the base of the gavel causing a continuous flow to the delightful thoughts of Casper hitting her inner bone. She suddenly screams out, "Casper this SHIT feels good. I'm Cumming"!! Casper suddenly responds, speaking quickly, "Jennifer, I got to go. A friend just walked in. I'll call you later Baby". Click. The friend walks in slowly and making eye contact says, "My turn"! Casper says, "That's what I have been waiting for Traci".

{Scene opens with Traci's head bobbing up and down on Casper's erected throbbing manhood.}

Traci raises her head to swallow the sweet juices flowing slowly from Casper's joy stick, as she softly speaks, "Casper, you need to leave that bitch alone". Casper, gently rubbing the wetness running down his inner muscular thighs, calmly says keep sucking baby, let your mouth speak good things to me. Traci spreads Casper's thighs open, while grasping his fudge sickle, deeply slurping all Casper's overflowing sweet milk. Traci pauses and glimpses at Casper, "I'm about to give you something that your high-class bitch can only wish about". Traci turns, while bending towards Casper's feet gliding back as the tip of Casper's one-eyed snake makes its way into the tight tunnel, pushing and wiggling down to his base, feeling the coarseness of his wet pubic hairs. Suddenly Casper's phone begins to ring in the background, Traci begins to bounce faster on his rod while yelling, trying to drown out the sound of his ringing phone, all while enduring the passionate pain of his long thick rod, "DO NOT ANSWER THAT BABY, THIS SHIT HURTS SO DAMN GOOD BABY".

Jennifer standing in the hall of the courthouse with a look of disgust on her face, while looking at her phone and speaking underneath her breath. I cannot believe him. Maurice, "let's go, we need to be in court, like now". Jennifer "I'm ready". She says, walking down the hallway at a fast pace, entering the courtroom. Maurice looks worried, "are you ok"? Jennifer, "Yes, I'm good"! The bailiff calls the court to order, "All rise", as the judge enters the courtroom and takes his seat, he grabs and slams the gavel. The Judge, an older white, slender, graying male with wiry hair, looking over his glasses, "You may be seated"!! Looking at Jennifer and Maurice, he asks, "Do you have anything to fortify your case with me"? Maurice replies, "Yes, Your Honor, we have evidence that this so-called Phantom has become a major player in the drug and prostitution ring. We also have his location, Your Honor. The judge, looking at Jennifer with great anticipation, proceeds, "So, what are you asking me to do"? Jennifer replies, "We're asking for a court order to tap any and all phone lines to track his every move, Sir". The judge considers for a moment, "Request granted! You have one month from today to present me with more evidence". Maurice, with excitement in his voice, "Thank You Your Honor. The judge again slams his gavel, "Court is adjourned"!

Taco, speaking to Casper on the phone, "You need to relocate six kilos to Belize by Wednesday". Casper replies, "Will do". Taco also adds, "And keep that Traci on a leash". Casper laughs out, "That's not a problem".

***{Scene opens with Casper and Traci arriving to
Maurice's pool house during the tropical storm.}***

Casper unlocks the door, "Damn, I'm drenched". Traci closes
the door, "Me too baby! I'm a mess". Casper looks at Traci, "No
baby, you're beautiful as ever". Casper reaches to turn on the
lights as Traci proceeds to the mirror, while removing the once
stylish golden Brazilian wig. Casper, looking at Traci says,
"I need to get out these wet clothes". Traci turns and looks
at Casper with a smirk, "Need some help"? Casper smiles,
"Later baby, I need to check my messages, we're already behind
schedule". Traci laughs, "well you check your messages baby,
I'm about to take a shower and find something dry to put on".
Casper begins to remove his white rain stained shirt, his black
pants and black silk boxers, while grabbing a yellow beach
towel from the hall closet. Traci turns on the radio and proceeds
to the shower. Casper opens the steamed filled shower, "Here
baby, I brought you a towel". Traci teases, "You sure you don't
want to join me"? Casper closes the door in silence, shaking
his head, and smiles while walking back to the living room to
listen to his messages.

{Maurice and Jennifer arrive to his gated Mansion as the storm begins to ease.}

Jennifer, with the look of amazement, "Why are we at Casper's house"? Maurice quickly turns his head towards Jennifer, "Casper's house"? Jennifer confirms, "Yes, I was here a few weeks ago, for a cookout". Maurice, with a look of disgust, while trying to remain calm, informs her, "No Jennifer, this is my house". Jennifer mumbles under her breath, "Damn you Casper"! Maurice parks the car and reaches for his umbrella in the backseat and runs to open Jennifer's door. Once inside the house Maurice tells Jennifer to make herself at home. Jennifer sighs, "I don't know how to repay you". Maurice smiles, while escorting her into his kitchen, "are you hungry"? Jennifer says, "No but a glass of wine would be nice". Maurice turns to his stainless-steel refrigerator to retrieve some chilled wine. Jennifer turns toward the big patio window as she looks at the calming storm, when she spots the pool house.

Casper, sitting on the black leather couch, looking through his messages, when his thoughts reflect on Jennifer listening to smooth jazz as he reminisced on how she clutched his broad chocolate shoulders as he thrust his manhood deep into her tight, moist garden. Her body gliding upward against the wall from his forceful, deep, passionate thrusting, as he speaks out loud to himself, "Damn! What have I done"? Traci enters the room at that very moment with a smile. "Yes, baby let's get it on". Casper jumps, realizing Traci has entered the room, "Not now baby"! Traci, not responding to his demands, lets the towel drop to the marble floor and bends down slowly towards Casper's opened muscled thighs and grabs his unaroused rod and begins to slurp the tip of his dick.

Jennifer, still staring at the pool house as she too reminisces on the passionate night she and Casper shared, is suddenly startled by Maurice. "Here's your drink". Jennifer quickly turns "Oh, Oh Thanks". Maurice, with the look of concern on his face, "Are You Ok"? Jennifer lies expertly, "Yes of course, just watching the storm pass".

***{Scene opens with Maurice standing behind
Jennifer as she looks as if she's in a daze,
looking directly at the pool house.}***

Maurice, "Let me find you something dry to put on". Jennifer turns and smiles, "Yes, I just need a hot shower and a soft bed". Maurice looks at Jennifer as if he's undressing her with his eyes, "Tell you what, let me fix you another drink first". Jennifer laughs, "Make it strong". Maurice tells her not to worry, "I have just what you need". Maurice turns the radio on before leaving the kitchen, Jennifer gazes back out the window, dropping her head with a look of sadness on her face, because the song playing is the same song her and Casper first made love to in the pool house. Suddenly, she opens the patio door as though she was hypnotized, Maurice returns to the kitchen looking surprised to see the patio door open. Maurice places the drinks on the patio table as he begins to grab Jennifer close to him, "Come here, and let me warm you up". Tears began to fall from her eyes as Maurice kisses her. Jennifer, looking shocked, "What are you doing Maurice, you know I'm dating Casper"? Maurice apologizes, "Please forgive me, I don't know what came over me". Jennifer pulls herself out of his arms. Maurice yells, "Damn It Jennifer, he doesn't love you, you need a real man like me". Jennifer is crying, as she yells back, "How do you know he don't love me"? Maurice grabs her around the waist and picks her up and kisses her passionately, as he takes her to his room. Meanwhile back at the pool house:

Casper is aroused, with Traci's wet lips and warm mouth gliding up and down his big veiny dick. Casper moans, "Damn Traci, you're going to make me cum". Traci slowly glides up his mountain top while swallowing the juices of saliva, "No baby we just got started". Casper flips her over while spreading and flickering his tongue into the rim of Traci's forbidden hole. Traci moans in the delight of his long-wet tongue entering forcefully back and forth. Casper growls, "I'm going to fuck the shit out of this tight ass".

{Back in Maurice bedroom}

Jennifer's back is resting on his black, plush satin pillows with her legs spread open like an eagle, ready to soar, as Maurice slurps her perky nectar as if was sucking a sweet ripe Georgia peach. Jennifer, pressing herself closer against his face, with her eyes rolling in the back of her head, "Oh Casper, Yes". Maurice begins to stick his finger deep inside her wet throbbing pussy, forcing her to cum in his mouth. Jennifer, still calling out to Casper, "This is your pussy baby". Maurice lifts her legs and enters himself with great force pumping at a hard and fast pace, causing her head to push against the headboard, making her pussy echo the sound of gushing juices hitting inside her tight walls, as Maurice pushes deeper and says, "before this night is over you will be calling my name". Jennifer calls out his name while grabbing onto his muscular rib cage, when she suddenly opens her eyes from the pleasure of the painful thrust and she realizes it is Maurice inside her. Maurice looks into her eyes, "Cum, cum with me baby". Jennifer pushes him off her, grabs the blanket wrapping it around her, as she runs down the stairs to the kitchen and pushes open the patio door, running towards the pool house. Then she notices the flickering light from the candles burning in the window and hears music playing along with the sound of moaning. She suddenly stops in horror, when she sees a man looking back at her with a big smile on his face. Casper, stroking Traci, as though he was an engineer driving without brakes, into a deep narrow tunnel about to crash. Traci busts out in a loud laugh, "BABY YOUR BITCH IS HERE". Jennifer screams out before fainting, "IT'S A MAN"!

***{Scene opens with Jennifer having lunch alone
in her office, when her phone rings.}***

Hello. Hello! Click. Jennifer appears unconcerned and continues eating when the phone rings again. Jennifer yells into the phone "Hello! Hello!" Click. Jennifer is now looking a bit puzzled when suddenly her office door opens. A female voice is speaking "Knock, knock it's me can I come in"? Jennifer smiles, "Get in here". Tyra says teasingly, "Well, well look who finally decided to come to work". Jennifer, with a slight smirk on her face, "I've been busy with another project". Tyra nods in agreement, "I bet you have". Both laugh out loud when the phone rings again. "Hello! Hello!" Click. Jennifer appears irritated. Tyra asks "what's wrong Jennifer"? Jennifer hunches her shoulder, "someone keeps calling but says nothing". Tyra seems just as puzzled as Jennifer, "Hmmm, that's odd, well let's get this meeting started".

Meanwhile, Casper is having lunch with Taco at Latitude's, an upscale steak & seafood restaurant in downtown Key West Florida. Taco, with a look of concern "Boss, what's going on between you and Maurice"? Casper slowly sips on his scotch, "Look Taco, that's not your concern". Taco sighs, "Ok, but whatever is going on it's affecting the daily operation". Casper leans forward, speaking slowly, "I Said it's no concern of yours. Understood"? Taco, with a look of shock replies, "Yes Sir, I understand". Casper continues, "Now back to what I called you here for". Casper cellphone rings, "Hello". A male voice says, "She's at her office". Casper answers, "I want to know her every move". The male voice replies, "I'm on it, Boss". Click. "Now, like I was saying, let's get down to business at hand". Taco reaches into his suit pocket and pulls out a white envelope. "Just as I promised Boss, the deal is done". Casper smiles as he places the envelope in his briefcase, "Very good, let's order".

Across town, Maurice is relaxing by the pool, talking on his cellphone with Candi. Maurice asks her a question he know the answer to "When was the last time you spoke with Pastor Dew Right"? Candi smiles and gasps, "Hmm, not lately, why"? Maurice says, "I think it's time for you and the good pastor to get reacquainted". Candi laughs, "Yes, I think it's time for a revival".

{*Back at Jennifer's office.*}

Tyra, fishing for answers, "Okay, now with the business out the way, what's really going on between you and Casper"? Jennifer, picking at her salad looks up, "Not a damn thing". Tyra sits back in the chair and fold her arms. "Girl, don't give me that bullshit, I've heard him in here fucking your brains out". Jennifer stands up, "That was then.... Oh Shit! Not again!" She grabs the garbage can and begins to gag. Tyra's eyes buck, when suddenly the phone rings again. Tyra answers. "Hello! Hello!" Click.

{Scene opens with Thanksgiving dinner being held at the breath-taking home of Casper and Maurice parents' home in Key West, Florida.}

Casper opens the door with a look of disgust on his face when he sees Maurice, "Hmmm, I see you're the first to arrive, huh"? Maurice replies, "I didn't think you were coming". Casper, not letting Maurice sour his mood answers "Not even the sight of you could keep me from coming today". Maurice begins to snicker when he notices Casper's date emerge from the den. "I see you brought a guest". Traci places his well manicure hand around Casper's waist, "I'm not a guest, and yes, I'm his woman". Casper kisses Traci's jaw, "Yes, we're a couple. Hope you can handle the excitement little bro". When the doorbell rings, Maurice turns to open the door. "Well, well, don't you look beautiful as always"? Casper and Traci gasp when Jennifer enters. Maurice smiles as he welcomes her in. He then glances at Casper, "Hope you can handle the excitement big bro". Jennifer, with a look of disgust, rolls her eyes at Casper and Traci, "Hello". Traci responds sarcastically to Jennifer, "Hoe". Maurice gently places his hand on Jennifer's back as he motions her into the living room. Traci quickly turn towards Casper, "now ain't that

21

bout a bitch'? Casper whispers, "Baby, don't let them upset you, and besides I'm with the one I love". Traci blushes as she pulls Casper close and embraces him with a passionate French kiss. A female voice "You've got to be kidding me". Casper quickly turns, "Mom it's ok, I want you to meet my girlfriend Traci". Mom, visibly upset by this, "Girlfriend"? Traci extends a hand, "It's so nice to finally meet you. I've heard so much about you Mom". Mom, standing with her arms folded, "That's funny, because I haven't heard anything about you. And that's Zara to you"

Meanwhile, in the living room, Maurice fixes a drink while Jennifer sits on the couch. Jennifer pouts, "I knew it was a bad idea for me to have come here today". Maurice tries to console her, "No Jennifer, it's Thanksgiving and I wanted you here with me. Despite everything we have so much to be grateful for". Jennifer nods her head in agreement, "I hope your parents like me". Maurice reassures her, "No need to worry, once they lay eyes on you they'll fall in love with you too". Jennifer bashfully smiles as Maurice sits next to her on the couch. "I hope you're hungry, because my mom's cooking is amazing". Jennifer laughs, "Are you kidding me? I'm so hungry I could eat a horse". Maurice laughs, "Well, knowing my mom I'm sure she could make a horse taste good". Jennifer laughs out loud as Zara enters the room, "Well, hello you two". Maurice stands and embraces his mom with a tight hug and kiss on her smooth chocolate jaw. "Mom, you look amazing as always". Zara smiles, "and who's this beautiful lady"? Maurice grins as Jennifer stands and extends her hand towards his mom "Hi, my name is Jennifer, so very nice to meet you". "It's a pleasure to meet you as well. My name is Zara," she smiles "but you can call me Mom". Maurice embraces Jennifer and his mom, "It's so good to be home". Jennifer asks Zara, "Is there anything I can help you with"? Zara smiles with delight, "Maurice, she's a keeper. Yes Jennifer, follow me to the kitchen".

Casper and Traci enter the living room as Jennifer and Zara walk towards the kitchen smiling. Maurice with a smirk on his face. "So, Traci, why don't you join the ladies in the kitchen"? Traci replies sarcastically, "Why don't you go to hell; besides I don't do domestic work"? A tall, handsome, older gentleman enters the room "There are my boys". Maurice and Casper respond at the same time "Dad"! Dad, noticing Traci, "and who's this lovely young lady"? Traci smiles as he responds "Hi, I'm Traci". Dad, with a look of surprise. "I'm sorry sir, please forgive me; I thought you were a woman". Maurice laughs hysterically as Casper holds his head down with a look of embarrassment. Traci responds with confidence "I'm transgender". Dad, still looking as though he saw a ghost, clears his throat "I'm Father Love, welcome to my home".

Zara returns to the living room with a look of accomplishment on her face. "Okay dinners ready; let's eat".

{Scene opens with Thanksgiving dinner ending and Zara is ready to serve desert.}

Zara smiles as she glances across the dinner table. "Hope you guys saved room for dessert". Traci quickly responds, "Oh Mrs. Bishop, let me help you". Zara slowly responds to Traci while looking at Jennifer, "Uh thanks, but no thanks. Jennifer, do you mind helping me in the kitchen"? Jennifer looks over at Traci with a smirk on her face, "Yes Ma'am, I would love to". Traci sighs as he mumbles under his breath as Jennifer and Zara walks toward the kitchen smiling. "Well I be damned"! Father Love clears his throat as he places the once white, crisp linen napkin onto his demolished dinner plate. "Well boys, while mom and Jennifer prepare dessert let's go to the balcony, we need to talk". Casper, Maurice and Traci rise from the table when Father Love quickly turns towards Traci, "Excuse me Ma'am, I mean Sir, but I need to speak to my boys in private". Traci plops back down in his chair, sighs and throws his hands up looking visibly disgusted as Casper quietly whispers, "It's ok baby, I'll be right back".

Meanwhile, in the kitchen, Zara and Jennifer are preparing dessert. Zara looks at Jennifer as she reaches for her hand,

"You're such a pretty and sweet young lady". Jennifer begins to blush and holds her head down in embarrassment. "Thank you, Mrs. Bishop". Zara reminds her, "No, please call me Mom". Jennifer, still blushing, replies, "Okay Mom". Zara continues, "You're exactly what Maurice needs in his life". Jennifer looks as though she saw a ghost and gasps "No Mrs. Bishop, I mean Mom, you don't understand. Maurice and I...". Zara interrupts her, as she places her hands over her mouth as though she is praying, "Jennifer, you are absolutely glowing".

Back in the dining-room Traci is sitting alone at the once blissful dinner table forking over his plate when the doorbell rings.

Out on the balcony, the men are overlooking the ocean view, as the sun begins to set and Father Love lights a Cuban cigar. "I called you out here to settle this feud between you two". Casper, with great anger in his voice, "I don't understand why we're having this discussion. Everyone knows I'm in charge". Maurice, looking visibly pissed speaking loudly as well "That's your problem now Casper, you think you know everything; and don't know SHIT". Father Love motions his hands as if he's seating the choir. "Now, now let's keep your voices down, you don't want Mother to hear you". Casper still visibly angry while pointing his finger at his chest, "It was me, and only me running this entire operation while Maurice's pretty-boy ass ran off to Harvard trying to impress you and Mom". Father Love replies, "Look Casper, yes Maurice went off to college, but only after clearing your ass from going to prison when you tossed that twelve-million-dollar shipment to an FBI informant". Casper becomes outraged and kicks a chair as he storms off into the house.

{Traci answers the front door.}

"Well if it ain't the Bobbsey Twins". Taco and Tara burst out in laughter. Tara snickers, "Traci, you're still a fool". Taco nods his head in agreement, when Casper enters through the den and shouts out to Taco, "WE NEED TO TALK NOW"! Traci and Tara, with a look of horror and shock, "What's going on"? Traci hunches his shoulders, "Girl it's been a trip all day". Tara asks, "Well, where's Aunt Zara"? Traci rolls his eyes and points towards the kitchen, "Girl she's in the kitchen with that trick bitch, Jennifer". Tara gasps, "Girl you got to be kidding me, I have got to see this one for myself". Traci throws his hands up again as Tara rushes off to the kitchen, "GREAT I'M ALONE AGAIN"!

Outside Casper is pacing back and forth smoking a cigarette shouting at Taco "IT'S TIME TO PUT PLAN B INTO MOTION"!

Tara enters the kitchen when she hears Jennifer talking to Zara. "Do you really think I'm glowing"? Tara gasps, "ARE YOU PREGNANT"?

{Scene opens with Zara directing her staff on where to place the Christmas tree, when suddenly her cellphone rings.}

"Hello". Jennifer recognizes the voice at once, "Hey Mother Bishop, is everything ok"? Zara, sounding concerned, "I'm not sure, I tried calling Maurice several times, but it just goes straight to voicemail. Have you seen him"? Jennifer hesitates before answering, "Uh, no ma'am I haven't seen or heard from him since Thanksgiving". Zara slightly gasps "Oh my, that's been over three weeks ago". Jennifer agrees, "Yes ma'am, but I'm sure he's ok". Zara, with a tone of concern, "Well are you ok? Are you taking care of yourself? Do you need anything"? Jennifer giggles softly, "Yes ma'am, I'm fine, just been a little under the weather". Zara hears the front door close and she looks towards the entranceway to the living room, "One moment Jennifer, I think I hear him now". Maurice enters the room looking like a model from a GQ magazine, wearing a black Armani suit while holding a dozen white orchids. Zara looks surprised and relieved all at the same time. "Maurice"! Maurice walks to her and slightly bends over to kiss her smooth caramel cheek, "Hi Mom". Zara, with a look of satisfaction while speaking back to Jennifer and hitting Maurice as if she was spanking him, "He's here Jennifer". Maurice laughs as he tries to dodge his mother's playful love taps. "OK, OK, Mom I'm sorry". Jennifer smiles while rubbing her stomach.

Meanwhile, across town, Casper's looking out his penthouse window that overlooks a sea of blue flowing water while talking to Taco. Traci is sitting Indian-style on a black leather couch blowing his manly, wet, freshly polished fingernails. Casper says to Taco, "Today is the day". Taco questions Casper, "Are you sure you want to go through with this Sir"? Casper raises his voice in anger, "HELL YEAH, his ass will die today". Taco know better than to question him a second time, "O.K. Sir. Well, I better call Father Love now to setup the meeting". Casper orders, "Make sure you sound convincing and be sure to tell him that I want to make amends with him and Maurice". "Okay Sir got to go". Casper hangs up.

Back at the Bishop's household, Father Love is in the kitchen making a sandwich, when his cellphone rings. "Hello". Taco puts the plan in motion, "Yes Sir, I have great news. Casper has come to his senses and wants to apologize to you and Maurice. He would like to meet at the gun range for a few rounds, just like the old days". Father Love smiles while licking mayonnaise off his fingers, "Sounds great, but why didn't he call me"? Taco chuckles, "That's Casper for you Sir". Father Love laughs out loud, "I guess you have a point. I think I heard Maurice in the living room with Zara, so I'll let him know as well". Taco adds, "That'll be great, Sir. We'll see you guys at 3pm". CLICK.

Meanwhile, in the living room, Zara's still talking with Jennifer when Father Love walks into the room. Zara has come up with a great idea, "Let's do dinner today"! Jennifer hesitates but Zara quickly interrupts Jennifer before she could answer while rolling her eyes at Father Love and giggling, "No is not an option; see you at 3pm". CLICK. Father Love smiles as he shakes his head, "Playing matchmaker again, my love"? Zara hits his arm and laughs, "It's called a mother's intuition, and besides she reminds me of myself". Maurice enters the room looking curious, "Who reminds you of yourself, Mom"? Zara sarcastically respond, "My daughter in-law Jennifer". Father Love smiles as he drops his head while placing his hand on Maurice's shoulder. "Don't fight it son. Your mother has a way of predicting these things, and besides we have a date at the range with your brother. It's his way of apologizing". Zara displays a huge grin, "Oh that's great; let's make it a party".

Returning to Casper's penthouse, Traci is looking visibly excited "Baby, I can't believe this is finally going to happen". Casper smiles, "I told you that one day I would be the king of this operation". Traci's excitement cannot be contained, "Let's go baby, I don't want to waste another minute".

It's 3pm and everyone arrives like clockwork. First, Jennifer is greeted at the front door by Zara and whisked off to the kitchen. Next, Casper and Traci arrive and are met with hugs and a high-fives from Father Love and Maurice as they walk towards the den for a celebration drink. Finally, Taco and Tara arrive in his Black Cadillac Escalade, before being escorted to the den by the maid. Tara, looking for her aunt, "where is Aunt Zara"? Father Love points towards the kitchen. "I'm Sorry for acting like an Ass". Maurice embraces Casper with a hug, "It's Ok Bro". Father Love motions his head towards the front door, "It's in the past son. Let's get to the range". Everyone is getting to ready to leave when Casper suddenly pauses, "Go ahead I'll be there in a minute".

The ladies are in the kitchen laughing and talking like old girlfriends. Zara says, "Ladies let's take this party out to the patio". All of them agree and they proceed to walkout. BOOM!!

{Scene opens at Keys Medical Hospital Key West, FL. ICU waiting-room, where Casper and Traci are sitting on the couch looking as though they were watching a movie, Jennifer is visibly upset, crying as Tara tries to console her. Taco quietly walks out of the room with his cellphone in hand, while Zara is speaking with the doctor who's caring for her husband and son.}

Zara takes control of the situation and says, "Okay, give it to me straight, and don't leave out any details". Dr. Jack Flop is very blunt, "Well, their condition is very grave at this time". Dr. Hoax is just as blunt, "Have you discussed organ donation with your family"? Zara, with a look of anger, screams at him, "YOU GOTTA BE KIDDING ME? You speak as though he is dead". Suddenly, a woman's voice comes over the intercom. "CODE BLUE! CODE BLUE"! Both doctors turn to answer the call. Zara grabs Dr. Jack Flop by the arm, "Don't forget I'm paying you very well". Dr. Hoax nods, "Understood"!

Taco is speaking in a soft whisper on his cellphone, "I think you need to come home right away". He is speaking to a yet unknown young female, "Why? What's wrong"? Taco doesn't want to say over the phone, "I'll have the jet waiting for you at the airport, I'll explain everything when you I pick you up". Click.

Back in the ICU waiting room a nurse enters the room to speak to the family. The nurse, as comforting as she can be, says "Your loved one has lost a large amount of blood and is going to need a blood transfusion. Unfortunately, Maurice has a rare blood type". Zara steps up, "Say no more, he's my son so I'll donate". Casper, with a look of dismay, "He's my twin, shouldn't I be the one to donate"? Zara puts her foot down, "Absolutely Not"! Casper angrily grabs Traci by the hand, "Let's get the hell out of here". Zara rolls her eyes at Casper as she turns to the nurse, "Let's go". The nurse tells her to follow her.

Driving on Highway 95, Casper's driving like at bat out of hell, while Traci braces himself with a look of fear. "Baby, slow down before we end up in the hospital too". Casper is irritated, "I'm going to get to the bottom of this shit today"! Traci is confused, "Get to the bottom of what baby"? Casper tries to explain, "She has always treated me differently than Maurice". Traci can tell no that Casper is angry, "Calm down babe, we're finally going to get everything we've dreamed of". Casper, with a scary determination says, "That's why I need to find my father's will".

Back in the ICU waiting room Jennifer and Tara are talking when they are interrupted by Taco entering the room with a young lady, leaving them with a look of total surprise. Tara speaks first, "Amber"? Amber replies, "Hi Cousin Tara, any news yet"? Tara drops her head, "It's not looking very good". Taco realizes there are a few people missing, "Where are Casper and Aunt Zara"? Tara thinks for a moment, "Aunt Zara is donating blood and Casper left". Amber, with tears in her eyes now, "When can I see Daddy and my brother"? Zara walks into the room and sees Amber, "MY BABY'S HOME". "Mom are they going to be okay"?

Meanwhile back at the parents' home, Casper and Traci are furiously looking through Father Loves study, trying to find his will. "Baby do you think it's here"? Casper isn't sure where it is, "I don't know, just keep looking". Traci suddenly comes across an old faded picture of a woman holding a baby attached to a birth certificate, "THIS JUST CAN'T BE TRUE"! Casper, looking anxious, "WHAT CAN'T BE TRUE"? "I don't know how to tell you this baby, but", Casper snatches the papers and drops onto the plush leather chair, "OH SHIT. I'M ADOPTED".

Back at the hospital, the family is faced with the devastating news from Dr. Jack Flop, "Mrs. Bishop, we've done all we could, but your son injuries were much too traumatic, and unfortunately, he didn't make it. I'm so sorry for your loss, and I know it's a bad time to ask but would you consider donating his organs"? Jennifer drops to the floor and faints, Amber screams out in sorrow, Tara looks as though she saw a ghost, Taco rushes to Jennifer's aid. Dr. Hoax is licking his lips as if he's about to delight himself in a five-star meal. All of this is happening while Zara rushes out towards Maurice's room. When she arrives to the room she sees Dr. Flop administering an unknown solution into Maurice's IV bag. Zara whispers, "HURRY BEFORE SOMEONE SEES YOU".

{Scene opens at Keys Medical Hospital
I.C.U in Key West Fl.}

Amber is crying historically, "Mama, why"? Zara calmly says, "Amber be strong baby, we will get to the bottom of this". Amber is still so confused, "but Mom not Maurice, he would never hurt anyone", as she falls to her knee's in front of the doors entering the hospital morgue. Dr. Flop's attention is drawn to Amber, "are you OK ma'am?" as he bends to help her up. Zara blocks his way, "I've got her Doctor. You've done everything possible to take care of my child. Please make sure the body is ready to be picked up and taken to the funeral home". Suddenly two unknown well-dressed men exit the elevator. "Excuse me ma'am we need to conduct an additional investigation before he can leave the hospital". Zara places her hand on her slender hip and asks, "Who are you to stop me from taking my son's body"? One of the unidentified males answers as tactfully as he can, "Ma'am you have our deepest condolences. I'm Officer Cornelius and this is my partner Mark. We just need to ask you a few questions and take some samples before you can have his remains".

Meanwhile, in Father Love's hospital room, Taco is hovering over Father Love's body as he rests under a drug induced coma. Taco, thinking he is alone, "I'm sorry I didn't know that it was going to happen this way". Jennifer overhears him, "what do you mean Taco"? Taco with a look of shock, "Oh, I didn't see you Jennifer, you startled me. I was just stating that I did not want something like this to happen on my watch. I was supposed to protect them against everything". Jennifer becomes emotional as she speaks, "I can't believe he's gone, I want whoever did this to pay Taco and I mean with their life"! Taco, who has never heard Jennifer utter an unkind word, says "You can't mean that Jennifer. Remember that you're a lawyer". Jennifer doesn't care what she is, "FUCK BEING LAW ABIDING". Taco agrees with her, "Jennifer, you're right, they need to be dealt with by me".

Back at Father Love's estate, Traci and Casper are in Father Love's office. Traci, eager to leave, "Casper, now that we have found what you needed let' go". Casper, still outraged, "NO DAMN IT! I PLAN TO DESTROY ALL OF THEM"! Traci, looking confused, "Well what are you planning to do with your father's things"? Casper jumps back as he grabs his chest, "Damn Isabel, I didn't expect anyone to be in today, especially after what happened to my father". Isabel glances at Traci as she leans closer to Casper, "I came in to straighten everything up for your mother's return". She then spots Father Love's secret safe open, "But why is your father's office in shambles, DID SOMEONE BREAK IN"? Casper expertly steers her toward the door, "Let's go talk, Isabel". Traci becomes visibly upset and begins to yell, "AND WHERE THE FUCK ARE YOU GOING WITH THE FUCKING MAID"? Casper calmly grabs Isabel around her waist, "I'll be right back, so please clean this mess up before my mother gets back home". Casper walks Isabel down the hall to the guest-room, "Ok baby let me explain everything to you. Isabel, I'm tired of hiding behind this mask, I have needs too". As she begins to unbuckle Casper's pants she lowers herself down onto his already throbbing dick.

***{Scene opens inside the empty ICU room in Key West
Medical Hospital. (Detective Cornelius Brown)}***

"Thank you, ma'am, for your assistance and please except
our deepest condolences on your loss". Zara with a look of
disgust, "I will get to the bottom of this, you can best believe
that detective". Detective Brown can see the fury in her eyes,
"Ma'am, please let us figure this out before you do something
you will regret". Zara, pointing her finger in his face, "Officer,
there's nothing I will regret about anything. I will do AS I
DAMN WELL PLEASE"! She walks away from the detective
as Dr. Hoax enters the room and he gently places his hand on
her shoulder, "Your son's body has been released and we will
have his personal items ready in a few minutes, we just need his
wife to sign if that's possible". Zara raises her voice, "Excuse me
doctor he's not married. I will sign for his personal belongings".

Meanwhile back at the mansion, Isabel's sexual moans echo
throughout the hallways, "Casper Yes, Yes, baby, please open
me up, I've missed you baby". Suddenly, a forceful banging
causes the bedroom door to shake, "WHAT THE FUCK IS
GOING ON? CASPER, I KNOW YOU GOT THAT BITCH IN
THERE". Isabel continues to grip Casper's waist as he thrusts

slowly and deeply inside her, as she calls out, "No Baby, don't stop, go deeper". Casper pounds her with the rhythm of Traci's knocking, "Whose pussy is this baby"? Isabel screams out, "IT'S YOURS BABY! IT'S ALL YOURS". Casper bites his bottom lip, while looking into her eyes as he presses deeper inside her, slowly thrusting his dick deep into Isabel.

Traci's continuous banging forces the door open and Casper quickly jumps up, reaching for his pants to run and stop Traci from leaving, "Traci Wait"! Traci is beyond angry now, "You Bitch, how could you do this to me, Casper? You will pay dearly for this"! Casper, answering sarcastically, "AND WHAT ARE YOU GOING TO DO TO ME BITCH"? Traci flashes the documents in his face. This just outrages him, "Bitch give me those papers and get the fuck out of here". Traci angrily tries to slap CASPER, when suddenly he grabs her hand as they began to tussle and Casper draws his hand back and slaps Traci to the floor as he snatches the papers from her hand. Traci, holding her face, "I HATE YOU"! Casper replies, "Shut your ass up and get out, Traci, go back to that little hole of a bar I found you in". Traci quickly picks herself up from the floor grabbing her stuff as she cries out "I THOUGHT YOU LOVED ME". Casper laughs, "BITCH PLEASE; YOU WERE JUST A MEANS TO MY METHOD". Traci rushes down the stairs and slams the door. Back in the bedroom, Isabel is standing on the balcony with a white satin sheet covering her, while watching Traci speed off in her black Lamborghini. She feels the sheet being pulled off of her? It's Casper, standing behind her, gently bending her over the balcony rails as he begins to enter his manhood deeply into her ass.

Scene opens outside Father Love's hospital room at Key West Medical Hospital, with Zara and Amber preparing to break the news about Maurice passing. Zara gently wipes Amber tears,

"Sweetie we have to be strong for your dad, he's still very weak". Amber nods in agreement as she takes a deep breath, "Ok"! Zara reaches for Amber's hand, "We will get through this as a family", as she too takes a deep breath.

Meanwhile, on Highway 95, Traci is parked on the side of the road while yelling in her cellphone, "THAT MOTHERFUCKER IS AS GOOD AS DEAD"! A mysterious female voice hastily responds, "WHO GIRL, WHO"? Traci replies in an icy tone, "CASPER"! The female voice tries to console Traci, "Girl, calm down, and give me the scoop". Traci, looking visibly upset, begins to explain.

Back at the hospital, Zara leans over and kisses Father Love on the forehead, causing him to quickly open his eyes. Father Love, speaking in a whisper, "Honey, how's Maurice"? Amber trying to hold back tears, "Hi daddy". Father Love bucks his eyes, "Amber"! Zara gently places her hand on his chest, "It's okay baby, just relax". Father Love, trying to raise up, "What's going on? Somebody tell me something". Zara does not wish to tell him anything right now, "It's okay baby, just relax, I'll tell you everything". Amber places her hand on Zara's shoulder, "Baby, Maurice is resting peacefully". Father Love takes a deep sigh, "Honey, you had me worried. I don't know what I'll do if lost my son". Zara turns to Amber, "let your father rest".

Back on Highway 95, Traci is still in an uproar. The female voice says, "Stay right there, I'm on my way". Traci agrees to wait, "Hurry up! Or I'll take care this shit by myself".

***{Scene opens with Casper and Isabel making
passionate love on the balcony....}***

Isabel arches her back as she pushes her pelvis closer into
Casper's erect joystick, "Oh Casper please, please, go deeper
baby. This has always been your destiny. DAMN!!! Please don't
stop". Casper grinds deeper, "SHIT! This pussy is so DAMN
good. Isabel, Oh baby, I'm cumming"! Casper gently lays Isabel
down on the plush bear carpet. "Damn baby, I feel as if..."
Casper hesitates as he sees a glimmer of headlights turning into
the driveway, "let's go inside baby"! Isabel notices a shift in
Casper's mood, "what's wrong"? Casper hastily carries Isabel
into the house, "Stay here baby. I'll be right back". Isabel, looks
puzzled as she watches Casper rush to put his pants on, when
suddenly they hear Traci's voice, "I KNOW YOU AND THAT
BITCH ARE STILL UP THERE"!

Meanwhile at the hospital, Father Love asks Zara, "When
can I see Maurice, baby". Zara tells him, "Soon baby, soon".
Amber comes rushing into the room in a rage, "Mama, come
here quick"! Zara is confused, "What's wrong"? Amber
whispers to her mother, "It's Jennifer, she's sick". Zara looks
worried, "Okay"! She quickly turns to Father Love, "We'll be

right back baby"! Zara kisses him on the forehead and dashes out of the room. "Amber where is she"? Amber tells her, "she's in the bathroom. Mamma is she...."? Zara know the rest of the question, "YES"! Amber is even more upset now, "You mean Maurice was going to be a father"?

Back at the Mansion, all hell breaks loose when Casper sees Traci and her girlfriend rushing up the stairs. Traci is armed with a gun and her girlfriend is waiving a bat. Casper screams, "BITCH! YOU BETTER KNOW WHO THE FUCK YOU'RE FUCKING WITH"! The girl with the bat says, "Just shoot that motherfucker". Suddenly, the bedroom door swings open "GET BACK IN THE ROOM"! The door slams shut, "Naw, let that bitch come out too"! Casper reaches for the gun, "OKAY BITCH, YOU DONE FUCKED UP NOW"! BANG!

***{Scene opens at Key West Medical Hospital
with Zara, speaking with Amber and Jennifer
outside Father Love's hospital room.}***

"I need you ladies to wait here while I break the news to Father". Amber looking visibly shaken, "Mom please, let me go in with you". Zara wants to do this alone, "Absolutely not, I need you to stay with Jennifer". Jennifer gently grabs hold of Amber's hand, "Your mom's right, let's do as she says". Zara takes a deep breath as she walks into the room, "Hey Baby". Father Love can see worry in Zara's eyes, "How's Jennifer"? Zara smiles, "She'll be just fine, baby". Zara leans in to hug Father Love as she whispers into his ear, "Everything is going to be alright, but need you to flow with me okay"? Father Love nods his head hesitantly, as Zara walks towards the door.

Back at the mansion, Casper and Traci continue to struggle for the gun, when suddenly, Casper accidently pulls the trigger, and shoots through the bedroom door, causing Isabel's loud screams to echo throughout the hallway. Traci and her girlfriend quickly turn and run down the staircase, leaving Casper standing in the middle of the hallway looking frightened.

Meanwhile on Highway 95, Taco and Tara are in route to the hospital to visit with their uncle, Father Love, when Tara receives a phone call from an unidentified person. Tara answers, "Hello"! The unidentified voice says, "I need to talk to you right away". Tara quickly tries to end the call, "I'll call you later, I can't talk right now". "DON'T HANGUP; EVERYBODY IS NOT YOUR FRIEND". Click. Tara turns to Taco looking puzzled. Taco reads her perfectly, "What's wrong"? Tara shares her confusion, "Something is just not right with this entire situation with Maurice and Casper". Taco agrees, "Yes, I know Sis, but now is not the time to let our emotions get the best of us, Uncle Love and Auntie Zara need us now more than ever".

Back in the hospital room, Zara is preparing to tell Father Love about the passing of Maurice. She speaks softly, "Honey, there is something important that I need to talk about". Father Love, looking nervous and confused, "What is it"? Zara slowly sits on the side of the bed and grabs Father Love's hand, "Maurice is no longer with us". Father Love squeezes Zara's hand as he begins to cry uncontrollably, "Baby, please tell me I'm dreaming". Zara tries to comfort him, "I wish it was a dream baby, but we need to start making plans for his funeral". Just then, the Doctor enters the room, "Mrs. Bishop, may I please speak to you for a moment"?

*{Scene opens at Key West Medical Hospital where
Zara, Jennifer and Amber are standing around
Father Love's bedside consoling one another.}*

Amber is crying uncontrollably, blaming herself for Maurice's death. "Baby Girl, it's not your fault". She disagrees, "But daddy, had I not went away to school, maybe I could have helped the family". Zara interrupts Amber, "Trust me, when I say, that everything is going to be alright". Jennifer runs out of the room yelling, "BLAME ME"! Zara rushes after her. Meanwhile Tara and Taco arrives to the hospital parking lot when they both notice Father Love's Chauffeur trailing behind a funeral service car. Tara, looking visibly shaken, "Oh no, Taco, we're too late"!

Back inside the hospital Zara is hugging Jennifer. "Jennifer, I promise, everything is going to be okay, but I need you to calm down for the sake of the baby". Jennifer, looking puzzled, "I don't understand, you have not shed a single tear". Zara tells her in the strongest way she can, "I don't have time to mourn, I'm too busy trying to keep my family together. Now I need to go back and get Amber so I can get you ladies home". Zara returns to the room to find Amber curled up with her father. "Honey, I'm going to take the girls home so you can relax, before Taco and

Tara arrive, and I want you to pay close attention to everything Tara says Okay"? Zara leans over and kisses him softly on the lips as she winks her eye.

Later, when the ladies arrive home Zara notices the front door is wide open. "That's strange"! Once inside, Amber proceeds upstairs to her room. Zara turns to Jennifer, "Now, as for you young lady, I'm going to give you something to relax, but first let me find Isabel so she can prepare your room". Jennifer, wishing to not be too much trouble, "Mama Zara, can I please stay in the pool house? I'll feel closer to Maurice there". Zara eyes buck as she stutters for words, "Uh, Uh, I don't think that'll be a good idea. I would rather you stay here in the main house". Jennifer tries to reassure her, "I'll be fine; I really need to feel close to him and if I should need anything, I will call you". Defeated, Zara agrees, "Okay, just let me get something to help relax you".

Later at the pool house, Jennifer quickly awakens out of a deep sleep when she hears a loud noise, "Who's there"? The curtains begin to wave from a strong ocean breeze. Then, she thinks she sees a shadow of what looks like Maurice and she gasps. "What in the hell was in those pills"? As she sits on the side of the bed, trying to gather her thoughts, she hears Maurice's voice, "I love you baby". Jennifer quickly rushes to the front door, "Don't be afraid"! Jennifer, looking visibly shaken, "I MUST BE HALLUCINATING"! Then she sees Maurice, and faints into his arms. The figure gently picks her up and lays her onto the bed, "I love you, baby"! Jennifer whispers, "This can't be real". He gently spreads her legs and begins to wash through her body like a child licking a Popsicle, Jennifer grips the sheets with an arch in her back, as she cums to the delight of his tongue, tingling inside her. "Let me make you remember what's forever yours". Jennifer wraps her legs around him as she gives in to his hostile takeover. As he inserts his gavel deeper and deeper inside her wet throbbing walls, she yells out, "THIS FEELS SO REAL!" as a tear falls from her eye.

Suddenly the bedroom door swings open. Amber screams out, "YOU'RE ALIVE"!?!